Tundra Books, an imprint of Penguin Random House Canada Young Readers,
a Penguin Random House Company

Library and Archives Canada Cataloguing in Publication available upon request

Hardcover ISBN 978-0-7352-6267-6

Published simultaneously in the United States of America by Tundra Books of Northern
New York, an imprint of Penguin Random House Canada Young Readers,
a Penguin Random House Company

Originally published in 2016 by Edizioni Lapis, Rome, Italy
This edition published in 2018 by Tundra Books

Library of Congress Control Number: 2017938918

North American edition edited by Tara Walker and Peter Phillips
North American translation by Thames & Hudson and Debbie Bibo
The artwork in this book was rendered in tempera, pastels and digital collage.
The text was set in Superclaredon.

Printed and bound in China

www.penguinrandomhouse.ca

1   2   3   4   5   22   21   20   19   18

tundra | Penguin
Random House
TUNDRA BOOKS

PETRA

MARIANNA COPPO

tundra

Nothing can move me.

Not the wind.

Not time.

I don't go anywhere.

Everyone comes to me.

I am strong.

I'm a fearsome, fearless,

mighty, magnificent mountain!

"Is that a pebble?"

"Woof!"

Me? A *pebble*?

No way.

I'm an egg. A smooth and shiny egg.

I'm not any ordinary egg.

I am an egg of the world,

in a world of possibility.

Will I breathe fire?

Will I wear a tuxedo?

Whatever I become, I'm bound to be amazing!

"There's no room for rocks in my nest!"

Oh no, not again.

This is becoming a pattern.

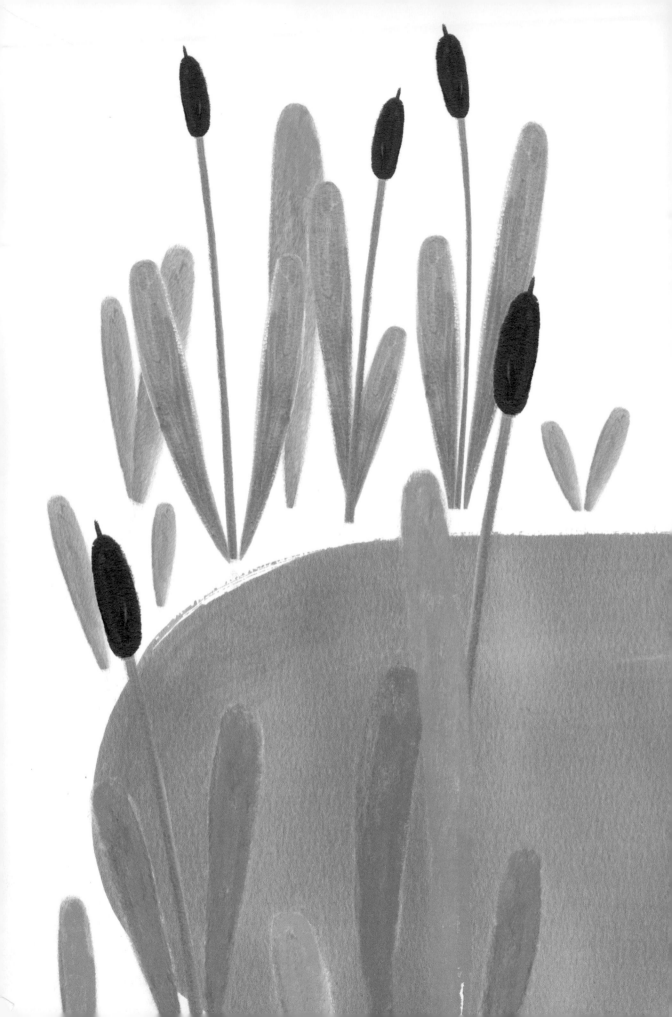

Well, they say no egg is an island . . .

But what an amazing island I am!

What paradise!

What palm trees, what peace, what sunshine, what —

"What a cool rock!"

Hmm, not bad at all.

What will I be tomorrow?

Who knows?

Well, no need to worry.

I'm a rock, and this is how I roll.